D1505220

TRANSFORMERS
EARTHSPARK

IT'S OPTIMUS PRIME TIME!

adapted by Patty Michaels

Ready-to-Read

Simon Spotlight

New York   London   Toronto   Sydney   New Delhi

SIMON SPOTLIGHT

An imprint of Simon & Schuster Children's Publishing Division
1230 Avenue of the Americas, New York, New York 10020
This Simon Spotlight edition August 2023

For information about special discounts for bulk purchases, please contact Simon & Schuster Special Sales at 1-866-506-1949 or business@simonandschuster.com.
Manufactured in the United States of America 0723 LAK
10 9 8 7 6 5 4 3 2 1
ISBN 978-1-6659-3951-5 (hc)
ISBN 978-1-6659-3950-8 (pbk)
ISBN 978-1-6659-3952-2 (ebook)

Meet Optimus Prime. He is a legend among Transformers robots!

Optimus Prime was born
on the planet Cybertron.
He is the leader of the Autobots.

For millions of years
he and the Autobots
battled Decepticons.

Optimus Prime battled the Decepticons, but his goal was never to conquer them.

His dream was always to bring peace to all Cybertronians. He believes that all beings should live in peace.

Like all Transformer robots, Optimus Prime has an alt mode. He can change into a semitruck. When he is a semitruck he can go much faster.

It is a clever disguise.
When he is in his alt mode,
he can go unnoticed since
the semitruck does not look
like anything out of the ordinary.

Optimus Prime also watches over
the Terrans, the first
Transformers robots born on Earth.
He is very protective of them.

The Terrans are young.
There is a lot they need to learn
about humans and other
Transformer robots.
Optimus Prime is grateful they
are part of the Malto family.

He also wants the Terrans
to know what it means to be a
Transformers robot.
He wants them to learn
from the very best!

Optimus Prime enlisted Bumblebee to be their trainer and teach them how to live safely as Transformer robots on Earth.

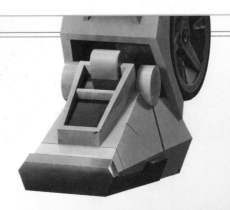

The discovery of the Emberstone
and the birth of the Terrans
have made Optimus Prime
hopeful for the future.

The Emberstone has life-giving powers.

GHOST AUTOBOT
ALLIANCE

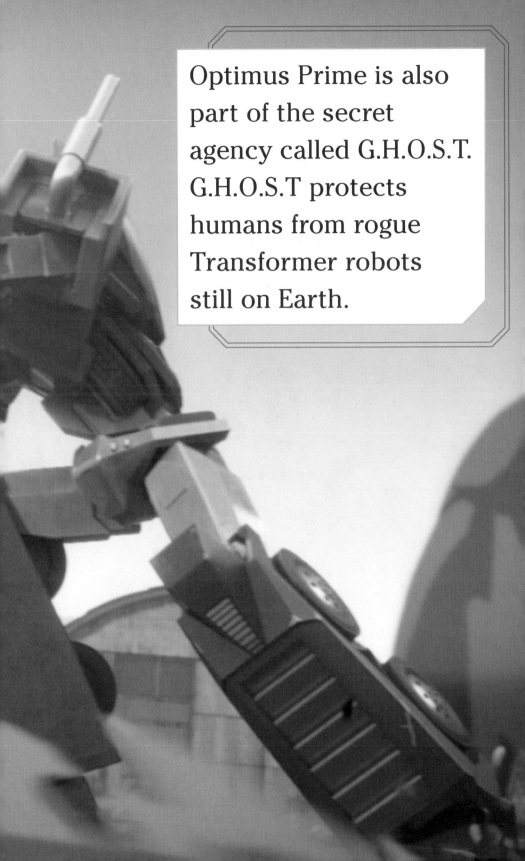

Optimus Prime is also part of the secret agency called G.H.O.S.T. G.H.O.S.T protects humans from rogue Transformer robots still on Earth.

Optimus Prime still works closely with other Autobots like Arcee, Bumblebee, and Wheeljack.

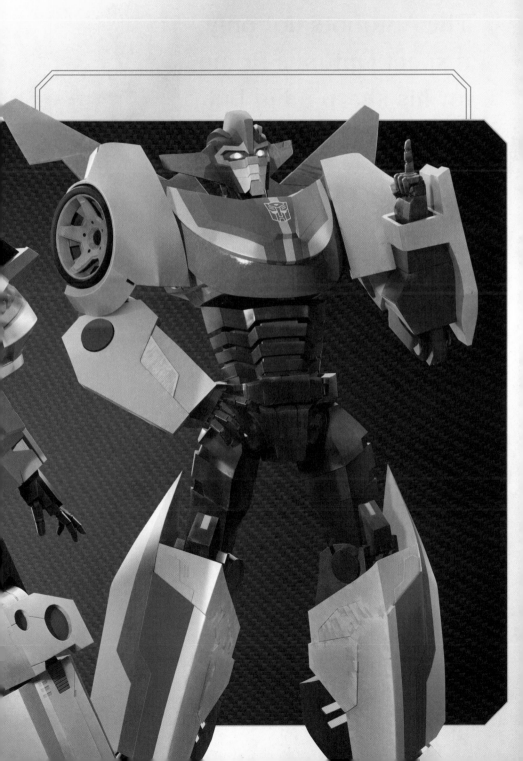

The Autobots not only respect Optimus Prime for his sharp mind but also his optimism.

When other Autobots
worry and lose hope,
Optimus Prime gives
them the strength
to carry on.
He is an inspiration!

Despite being strong, smart, and brave, Optimus Prime still needed a lot of help to end the Transformers War.

He joined forces with
his former enemy,
Megatron.

Megatron was once the leader of the Decepticons.

But to put an end to the Transformers War, Megatron gave Optimus Prime his oath to help the Autobots.

Although they have different leadership styles, Optimus Prime and Megatron have learned to work together.

Optimus Prime's greatest hope is that one day all beings—human, Autobot, Decepticon, and Terran—can live together in peace and make the world a safer place for everyone.

Every day he works hard
to turn that hope into a reality.

Thank you, Optimus Prime!